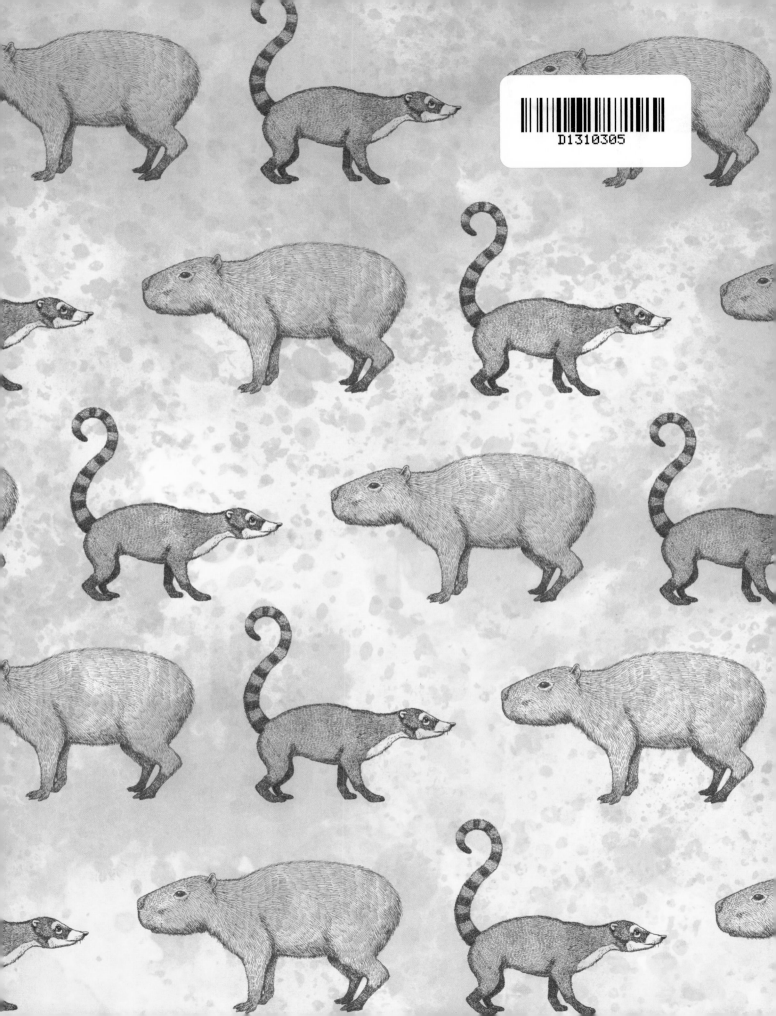

untitled

written & illustrated
by Timothy Young

I don't know, Carlos.
He didn't draw me with a watch.

Hey, Ignatz, what time is it?

Schiffer Publishing Ltd

4880 Lower Valley Road • Atglen, PA 19310

Library of Congress Control Number: 2018959883

Edited by Kim Grandizio

Type set in Fink/Kidprint/Noteworthy/Courier/Times

ISBN: 978-0-7643-5708-4
Printed in China

Published by Schiffer Publishing, Ltd.
4880 Lower Valley Road
Atglen, PA 19310
Phone: (610) 593-1777; Fax: (610) 593-2002
E-mail: Info@schifferbooks.com
Web: www.schifferbooks.com

For our complete selection of fine books on this and related subjects, please visit our website at www.schifferbooks.com. You may also write for a free catalog.

Schiffer Publishing's titles are available at special discounts for bulk purchases for sales promotions or premiums. Special editions, including personalized covers, corporate imprints, and excerpts, can be created in large quantities for special needs. For more information, contact the publisher.

We are always looking for people to write books on new and related subjects. If you have an idea for a book, please contact us at proposals@schifferbooks.com.

Dedicated to the absurdest comedy I grew up on; Looney Tunes cartoons, Marx Brothers movies, Monty Python's Flying Circus, Mad and Cracked Magazines, and comedians like Jonathan Winters, Steve Martin, and Steven Wright.

When do you think he's going to get started?

Beats me, I have no idea what we're doing here or what's going to happen.

Well, I think...Hey, Ignatz!

Weren't you a porcupine on the last page?

Yeah, now I'm a capybara.

I guess he changed his mind again.

Maybe he got tired of drawing all the quills.

I'll bet something is about to
happen that will make us angry.

He's done that in so many books.

Well, I'm not gonna fall for it.

Mostly I'm just bored so far.

I wish he'd send us on some kind of adventure to battle dragons or monsters or aliens or something.

It would be fun if he did something different;
like make us cowboys and set our story
in the Old West.

He'd probably be able to figure out
a title if he wrote a story like that.

Or maybe he could send us on an
undersea adventure.

I've never seen a book about a
coatimundi and a...wait, what are you again?

I'm a capybara, world's largest rodent.

He likes drawing lesser-known animals.

That would be cool. Knowing him, he'll probably throw
us into a scene from somebody else's book.

See what I mean.

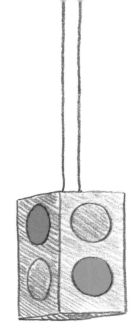

Yeah, you're right. He's a bit of a show-off that way.

I wish we had a better writer. There are so many good ones. It would be great to be in one of their books.

I know. With so many fantastically talented illustrators,
I'd love to be drawn by one of them!

I guess we're stuck in this book.

He hardly writes a story. He just relies on
characters like us to come up with the dialogue.

I don't think he's written a complete paragraph in his life.

OMG! When is something going to happen?

Did you really just say OMG?

Sorry, he made me say it.

You know what, we're almost at the end of
the book and I don't think anything
interesting is going to happen.

Well, I didn't see that coming.

He does like an ending with a twist.

Let's just hope he writes a sequel
and gets us out of here.